Up

Joe Cepeda

HOLIDAY HOUSE / NEW YORK

For the Licanos

I LIKE TO READ is a registered trademark of Holiday House, Inc.

HOLIDAY HOUSE is registered in the U.S. Patent and Trademark Office.
Printed and bound in April 2016 at Tien Wah Press, Johor Bahru, Johor, Malaysia.
The artwork was created with digital tools.
www.holidayhouse.com
First Edition
1 3 5 7 9 10 8 6 4 2

Library of Congress Cataloging-in-Publication Data

Names: Cepeda, Joe, author, illustrator.
Title: Up / Joe Cepeda.
Description: First edition. | New York : Holiday House, [2016] | Series: I like to read | Summary: "On a very windy day, a boy stands by a window with his pinwheel and is suddenly whisked into the sky where he can see a pig, a hen, a cow, and a sheep"— Provided by publisher.
Identifiers: LCCN 2015045420 | ISBN 9780823436552 (hardcover)
Subjects: | CYAC: Winds—Fiction. | Domestic animals—Fiction.
Classification: LCC PZ7.C3184 Up 2016 | DDC [E]—dc23 LC record available at http://lccn.loc.gov/2015045420
ISBN 978-0-8234-3689-7 (paperback)

Look.

Look.

I go up.

I see a hen.

I see a sheep.

I see a cow.

I see a pig.

They go home.

I go home.

Some More I Like to Read® Books in Paperback

Animals Work by Ted Lewin

Bad Dog by David McPhail

Big Cat by Ethan Long

Can You See Me? by Ted Lewin

Cat Got a Lot by Steve Henry

Drew the Screw by Mattia Cerato

The Fly Flew In by David Catrow

Happy Cat by Steve Henry

Here Is Big Bunny by Steve Henry

I Have a Garden by Bob Barner

I See and See by Ted Lewin

Little Ducks Go by Emily Arnold McCully

Me Too! by Valeri Gorbachev

Mice on Ice by Rebecca Emberley and Ed Emberley

Not Me! by Valeri Gorbachev

Pig Has a Plan by Ethan Long

Pig Is Big on Books by Douglas Florian

Pug by Ethan Long

Up by Joe Cepeda

What Am I? Where Am I? by Ted Lewin

You Can Do It! by Betsy Lewin

Visit http://www.holidayhouse.com/I-Like-to-Read/ for more about I Like to Read® books, including flash cards, reproducibles and the complete list of titles.